Crown

natasha carrizosa

CoolSpeak Publishing Company

Book and cover design by Carlos Ojeda Jr. and CoolSpeak Publishing
Company.

ISBN-13: 978-0-692-18688-6

crown (table of contents)

roots & rocks

(short stories/flash-fiction/prose)

Stretch Out

there was this one time. on fifth avenue. my momma opened our two-bedroom home to some abandoned children. abandoned like your parents are still there, but not really. abandoned like you think they have been swallowed by drugs, but you don't really know what that looks like. you do know what it feels like. feels like missing school, like matted, greasy hair. like wearing dirty clothes and torn up shoes. like they always laugh at you. like hunger. like crying. like being angry or sad all of the time. like when you do get to go to school, the other kids make you feel shame. they know you just came for the free lunch. ain't no field- trip money. ain't no permission slips or lunchbox. ain't no friends or teachers that care about you. abandoned like having no name. like being mad at GOD (if there is a GOD) for giving you a momma and daddy like them.

abandoned. like that.

like these kids were living in an abandoned house. down the street from us.

there were three of them. young, half-breed kids (like they used to call us.) two sisters, one brother. and, five of us. plus, my momma and daddy. how many is that? them three and us seven? that make ten.

ten living, breathing bodies in a two-bedroom apartment on fifth avenue. there has got to be something holy about that. (will GOD make room?) ten and two (bedrooms) make twelve. (tribe.)

my momma made room. she brought them babies in. said

something about they parents was grown. they couldn't
come in, but them babies could.

as a grown woman now, writing this story. this whatever it is.
i call them babies. because i know the violin strings of my
momma's heartbeat. because i know stretch. stretch self.
stretch a loaf of bread (give us this day.) stretch out like that
bologna and cheese. stretch a pot of beans and rice. stretch
that meat and potatoes. stretch them tortillas and refried
beans. stretch them food stamps. so, my babies can eat.
make it stretch. stretch out stretch out on a pallet. so, these
babies can sleep. stretch these arms. stretch out like
sacrifice. (like jesus help me.)

stretch out.

years later, now. sitting in the dark on this wooden bench,
truth is - i am so near cry. so near my momma nem. so near
these kids whose names i cannot remember. so close, i
know why. a mother of five would open my eyes. open
my/her heart/home up like a two-bedroom apartment.

i/we would never know abandonment.
home is where the heart is.

(are these words what GOD meant?) (is this what jesus
did?) (is this faith?)

feed the children.
in too small space.
(12 lives. 12 tribes.)
home. is where the heart is.
(see. GOD's face.)
this is my momma. what she did/i will do.
what HE is.
i am, too.

7

(have home/have faith.)
who feels it, knows it.

stretch out.

work. (write.) hard.

they called them the east side projects
i slept in a twin-sized bed with tati
i think she was two
we lived with isaac and his girl
at the time
(i think that was before the twins came)
i can't remember much of anything
besides working hard
and, writing
lines from poems/motivational quotes
on notebook paper
and, tacking them on the walls
that surrounded us

i got fired from my job at the dollar movies
i left an hour or two early one night
and, these two, young, black boys
stole hundreds of dollars
from a desk that didn't belong to me

i do remember
one came from a good home
the other
lived with his granny
somewhere off of miller

i did everything i could
to save them from jail
to recover the money
i lied to them and said
the cameras caught everything

there were no cameras

if there had been
they would have caught/captured
three young black kids
that were tired of being broke

i was never angry with them
or, the white men
that gave me my walking/freedom papers

i work (write.) hard
i can never forget
anything

life/money
memory/poverty
writing/working
struggling
(ink-filled tears)
streaming
remembering
thinking

in my head
(screams)
all of the years
(processing)

or

maybe i am living my dream?

question: natty, why do you write?

answer: writing is. how i process.
my feelings/thoughts/anxiety/depression/ptsd/mistakes
memories. my LIFE.

question: natty, how can/do you write so much?

answer: i am inspired by everything. i listen to music. it
chooses me. i try to capture myself. my students. my family.
my friends and enemies. the people. the stories. the places
that THE MOST HIGH sends me to. the things the world
forgets to remember/be grateful for. (i think/know i ended two
sentences in a preposition.)

question: natty, what is a preposition?

answer: something all of my english teachers said you
should never end a sentence in. (i did it, again.) the definition
of a preposition is usually a short word that shows the
relationship between two other nearby words. preposition
means positioned before.

question: can you give me an/some example(s)?

answer: absolutely.

above.
inside.
within.

11

i will use them in a sentence. so, you get the meaning. (we all are holy word. living. preposition. connecting. relationship.

but, first. let me ask you some questions.

are you drowning in sorrow/debt/doubt/thoughts?
search above.

do you run to others for answers/from yourself?
look inside.

are you self-medicating because you cannot swallow life's medicine/lesson? see within.

question: natty, do you have all of the answers?

answer: no. i just write. writing is. how i live.

a half job

i can't remember how young i was. but i was small. still
playing chutes and ladders. i remember that. one of the few,
if not only, board games me and my brothers had. i can see
the box. broken at the edges, but still housing so much joy.
me and my brothers were like that box. the housing joy part.
we loved to play. inside and outside. we were full of smiles
and autumn colors. so were the dishes. for some reason,
momma was in her life-teaching mood. fall out. shoot.

just shoot me now, i thought. kill all of my joy. i couldn't play
until i washed the dishes. there i stood. at the kitchen
counter. it ran across my narrow chest like some cruel
border. standing between me and time with my brothers. the
sink and counters full of a thousand plastic cups. dirty plates
and crusty forks. i will never finish this. even if i go fast. that's
it! go fast! i decided in my little girl wisdom, i'd just go fast.
and be done. just as soon as godzilla quit talking.

the water was running slow. the palmolive was oozing out of
the bottle like syrup. like it does at school. from these little
ketchup-like packs they give you. when we get waffles for
breakfast, the key is to fill every tiny square with one drop.
that takes so much time. the result is sweet. this washing
dishes mess was not that. it was torture. everything was
water-torture slow. the bubbles were taking their time.
momma was sounding like the grown-ups on charlie brown.

i was a prisoner of suds. i knew no one was coming to save
me. i'd have to liberate myself. go fast. wash the dishes. (just
wait until she walks off) and then you can play!

i did. i washed the dishes like i was possessed. raking the

soggy dishrag across the plastic cups. dipping the forks and spoons in the palmolive water and chunking them on the other side of the sink. i did the plates this way, too. in record time, i was done. just like that.

now! i could play. i didn't tell momma i was finished. i just eased out of the kitchen. i went to play. somewhere. anywhere but here with the dishes.

TASHA!

godzilla called me into the kitchen. smoke flaring from her nostrils. eyeballs wide and full of fire. i held my breath. waiting to be burned alive. (i knew why.)

i tried to defy her. i tried to be slick. she caught me. right by the back of my neck. i was getting that rise in my belly. like when you ride a roller-coaster. well, how i imagined it would be. we never got to ride roller coasters. but you know, that same feeling you get when you go over a hill. sitting in the last seat of the church/school bus.

no bus was coming for me. no daddy. no brothers. nobody was coming to save me. it was just me and godzilla standing at the kitchen sink. she was screaming through fireballs about what she asked me to do. something about 'her dishes' and grease. i knew i was going to get a whuppin'. brown kids get whuppins', white kids get spankings. or grounded.

i remember one time, in the middle of a whuppin' - i screamed and begged for her to ground me. one of my white friends in my brownie troop had gotten grounded. she stopped and asked - what?! grounded?! (i swear i heard her laugh at the idea.) i had lied to her about something. she thought about it for two seconds. picked up where she left off. and then, grounded me.

i knew better than to ask to be grounded. double punishment was for suckers. i was a fool, but no sucker. godzilla was still screaming. i was scared! do you hear me?

what would my fate be? no doubt, i'd have to go outside and pick my own switch.

momma took all of the dishes out of the tray. she ran more scalding-hot water. squeezed more palmolive out of the bottle. swished her hand in the water to make bubbles. and, gave me that momma look. (you know the one.) i was back to where i started. this time, she stayed by my side and watched me.

if you gonna do something, don't do a half job.

she showed me how to wash everything. dish by dish. plates. pots. forks. spoons. knives. she lined the cups up. she ran scalding hot water in one. picked it up and started pouring the smoking water into each of the others. (kinda like i did the waffles. drop by drop. but fast. she had much more experience than me.)

she placed the clean dishes in the tray to dry. wiped the counters and stove down with pine-sol. i watched her like God was revealing a secret. i loved her so much. i wanted to make her proud. she took one of the cups out of the tray. it was now dry. she rubbed her thumb on the side of it. it made a squeaky sound. (oh! squeaky clean. i get it.)

i got it. i took over after that. eager to really help momma. to show momma i could and would do it right. i would never do a half job again. at the kitchen sink or in life.

parenthesis :

1) either or both of a pair of signs ( ) used in writing to mark off an interjected explanatory or qualifying remark, to indicate separate groupings of symbols in mathematics and symbolic logic

2) the material contained within these marks

3) ----------

4) an interval

(choose) answer:

1) be believer

2) be beggar

3) both are gawd (holy)

(or/oar)

4) all of the above

write in the space below . . .

me and the bumble bee

i guess i have always been a writer. a creator. i have always loved the look and feel of words on paper. especially, if i put them there. even as a young child, i loved the art of writing.

this is a short story – one, i always wanted to write. this is the story of a five-year-old me and a bumble bee. it takes place on the hood of my grandmother's car. that old LTD was always parked out front of our four-plex on may street. it laid out on the rocky front yard like a magic carpet. it was an open door to my imagination. hadji and i played so many games in and around that car. hide and seek. the dukes of hazzard. we used to lock ourselves inside in the summer. pretend we were on our way to somewhere. sweating out dreams and secrets. i loved that car.

most days, after school i'd gather my pencils and papers. go outside and lay on the hood of my grandma's LTD. it was the color of a weather-beaten penny. the magic carpet was always waiting to take me for a ride. it always seemed to be warm and i felt safe there. i suppose it is a symbol of my youth. my first writer's desk. a fond memory of what would become my future.

the day is sunny. i've put in my time at de zavala elementary school. i have abandoned any chores or homework to go outside. to think and write. i'm scribbling words. like i know they will carry me somewhere. away. from my so young life. i have no troubles to escape. my life with my grandma is good. i miss my mother sometimes. but, she comes around every now and then.

back then, i do not understand my mother is like me - young.

and she has gone away to grow. i do not resent her. i love being where i am. everything around me is growing. the trees. the flowers. the children. the family. grandma florene is everything to everyone of us. provider. protector. patriarch. and she lets me, her first-born grandchild have free reign to be who i am.

i am enjoying this moment more than most days. i am young, but aware. i have to be. i am aware of the beauty that surrounds me. i am aware that silence, like nature, is comforting. writing is comforting. to me.

i don't remember what i was writing. i remember the plump, black and yellow bumble bee. buzzing so close i could hear its wings toying with gravity. i could see the fuzz on its small body. it would come close and fly off.

off and on it would dance near my ear. my hand that held the pencil. the paper that held my words. almost as if it wanted to know what i was writing.

i stopped writing to watch the bumble bee. it was so pretty. no. more than pretty. it was stunning. i laid real still. not moving at all. my right hand holding a yellow number two pencil. lead leaning on the white paper. waiting for the next word to come from me.

it was just us two. me and the bumble bee. i was mesmerized by its beauty. what it did next, i will never forget. i laid on the magic carpet perfectly still. the bumble bee flew closer to my hand. it landed on my thumb. and, just as i fell in love with this majestic thing, it stung me.

i watched the bumble bee push its stinger into my thumb. hard. like i pushed my pencil into paper. i was confused, at first. why did this thing hurt me? i did nothing to provoke or deserve such pain. but, more than that - i watched it hurt me.

my thumb immediately started swelling. the bee flew away. i gathered my things and ran into the house. my grandmother emptied the tobacco from one of her cigarettes. got some ice from the freezer. and made a salve for the throbbing pain.

i have written countless words since those magic-carpet-ride times. i have written past the memory of the bumble bee. but, that bumble bee taught me something.

writing stings. it can be beautiful and painful. it can be sweet, like surrender. or iron-hot like hell. but, a writer. a writer is like a child. full of imagination and truth. a writer never forgets the sting of the beginning.

and we chase the bee/BE the rest of our lives.

vision street

closed my 12-year-old eyes. at 11:11. on the bus with my friend B. made a long-forgotten wish. like he told us to. said something about this was the only time the clock looked like this. we must have been on a morningside/field-trip.

middle school was a trip.

we were vision street wear kids. (i got mine from the henderson street pulga. right by the bridge. they sold knock-offs for kids like us. (we just wanted to fit in. look like them. snow-white.) kids with black and brown daddies and mommas that waited/sacrificed for us. bated breath. healed us with sopa. no meat on the bones. rough times. Tough streets. skinny kids that always knew the way home. (dorotéa. just click your heels together.) corn tortilla kids/families that caught the bus to themselves on the weekend. (ruby-red/shamed face) traded and bartered for mexico. hansel pills for high blood pressure. arthritis. gretel documents that turned into fool's gold. rusted train cars. tin necklaces. popcorn. music. candy apples. big-top wool blankets with white wolves on the front. (speak, spirit.) velvet paintings of bull-fighters. zippo lighters. (for the dark people.)

i was a dark kid.

i wore black from the D.A.V.
didn't breathe too hard. wrote poetry.
hoped nobody saw me.

monkey. in the middle.

my soul was second-hand-stitched. held together by

refugee/vision street kids. kids named in kampuchea. B (big-bellied boy. that wore a blue and red striped shirt more than one day a week.) A (pronounced like - uh nail.) (sounds like/looks like angel.) (her body. hammered so young. by men they told us to stay away from.) M.E. (ó seá/see maria elena.) (elaine marie.) a white kid named D. (he was king. had a brick for a smile. these kids spoke my language. we were shakespearean actors. (they are still. etched. memory.) all the world's a stage. hamlet. juliet. taming of the shrew. they were me. seven ages. scarface. they knew. sacrifice. kipling. IF.

if only i knew what to do.
read. write. (11:11)
make a wish. with all your might.

if you can dream, and not make dreams your master.

ms. raven. poe.
memorize this word: pour.
morningside: door.

if you can think. and, not make thoughts your aim.

imagination celebration.
keeper of secrets.
second-hand culottes.
(to look like i came from money.)
to keep my legs warm.
(write/right when the lights get cut off.)

if you can meet with triumph and disaster.

refugee. in my own land.
representation.
of what GOD ought to do.

massey's on 8th avenue.
i chewed.
swallowed pride.
chopping block.
mouth open wide.
tic-toc.
chicken-fried steak.
life at stake.
don't look at the clock.

i landed.
on page.

(and treat those impostors just the same.)

wrote my way.
into sea/see
light:
candle.
meeks/vigil.
pacesetter.
poor/righteous/teacher.
(climb this hill.)
(just click your heels
together.)

they cut me. in half.
before my momma gave me a name.
before my daddies got their papers.
(two by two)
noah's ark.
(she smart.)

there's no place like home.

before i felt the horns.
before i hurt.
before i was aware of cross.
before i knew they believed my skin was a curse.
before i became. moses.
(cut her in half. see who cry. see who laugh.)
see: ram
before i knew the word: bully.

before i could see
i had vision

and so hold on when there is nothing in you
except the will which says to them:
hold on

the little house in the back

we lived in a small house tucked back behind fairmount street. it sat quiet, sheltered by young trees. there was a gravel driveway that led to the front door. inside of this small house lived a young family just taking root. it was me, momma, daddy, isaac, and a newborn pelos.

i was in the second grade. isaac was in kindergarten. on school days, momma and daddy were gone before the sun came up. i was in charge of getting me and isaac ready for school. and, pelos to mimi's house. i knew momma wanted to be there. i understood early on, she had to work. we all had to.

i had to walk isaac to school before my bus came. i was very careful. taking back streets for blocks. passing 6th and 5th avenue. when we reached de zavala elementary, i would watch isaac until he was safe inside. make the blocks back home. stand out in front of the little house on fairmount street. and, wait for the school bus to come carry me far away.

one day, before momma went to work on the city bus. she told me she wanted me to put a pot of neckbones on when i came home. i listened carefully. i wanted to do everything right. just like she would if she was there.

i can't remember if pelos was at mimi's or not. she was a cuban refugee. she had left her country to live in the apartment in front of us. she would sometimes babysit my baby brother. she had this loud, beauty full laugh. a perfectly picked out afro. she was in love with marlene. they lived together. she had also left cuba. they were just a couple.

people we loved and loved us. momma never judged. i
learned that from her.

home from school. bridge.

here i am in the kitchen. standing at the sink. rinsing the
neckbones for dinner. i washed them carefully a few times. i
put a big pot of water on to boil. it's heavy. my arms aren't as
strong as momma's. they/i will be. i season the meat with
salt and pepper. garlic powder. i even dice white onion, like
i've seen momma do. the neckbones are boiling. i turn them
down and put a top on the pot. and wait for the kitchen to
smell like it does when momma cooks.

i sit down at the kitchen table to do my 2nd grade homework.
isaac is somewhere in the small house when momma walks
through the door. she is late, but always on time. she comes
to the kitchen and finds me. i am peeking out from a book.
i'm a little nervous when she walks to the stove. she looks at
the pot and looks at me. she takes a fork and pulls out one
of the tender neckbones. she takes a bite and looks at me.

who helped you with this?

nobody, i reply.

her eyes are wide. slowly a wide smile breaks out from her
tired face. she is eating what my second (grade) hands
made. judging by her pretty face, it's good.

momma made some rice. when my family ate dinner that
night, i was so proud of myself. i did what momma did a
thousand times before. i cooked. i made something. maybe it
was nothing. maybe it was everything.

i will never forget that little house in the back.

like my father – a poet

i want to write you words that will heal the both of us. i don't know where to begin. i am full of wishes and dreams that will mend our hearts. take us back to beginning. or wherever we need to be. what does a daughter say to her father? to tell him that she loves him. to tell him that she forgives him. she forgives herself. for the lost time and stolen memories.

we are the lost and found poets. in love with silence. living our lives on blank page and empty canvas. always waiting on a poem or a painting to make us happy again.

i remember every moment we ever spent. together. when the rest of the world would fall away. when the past meant nothing. when the reasons why didn't matter. i was a child. you were a man. we both suffered. we both loved. we still do.

when i was ten, i wrote my first poem. i remember reading it to my mother. she said - your father writes poems. my father i almost never saw. my father i hardly knew. i knew from then, i wanted to be like you. i wanted to be closer to you. i wanted you to be proud of me.

when i was fourteen, you handed me a newspaper. in it, a poetry contest. i wasn't the poet. you were. you let me read your brilliant poems. you revealed yourself with paintings of pyramids. of the human body. of the mayan calendar. all things you pulled from your heart and painted. you shared your art with me like a secret. like a dream. like a birthright.

you smiled at me and encouraged me. i could. i could write a poem. i could dream. you loved me. and i knew. (i still do.)

(all a child needs is to know they are loved. nothing else matters.) i could enter the contest. i had nothing to lose. my fear was worth your approval. i wrote a poem. like you - my father, had many times before.

i forgot about it. until the letter came to my mother's house.

natasha carrizosa, we are pleased to inform you that your poem marked by simplicity has been accepted into the so and so anthology. your presence is requested at so and so hotel for a poetry reading. honoring all of the poets that contributed to this book.

or, something like that. i read that letter a hundred times. i couldn't believe it. i was so happy. i was proud of myself and my words. i am smiling now. remembering my name on that letter. the name of my grandmother. the name of my father. the name you gave me. carrizosa.

i couldn't wait until i saw you again. i wanted more than anything for you to read that letter. to smile at me. to be proud of me. to know. i was like you - my father. a poet. no matter what.

i am fighting tears now. like i did many moments in my childhood. when we were just miles away from each other. but, couldn't see each other. the why doesn't matter anymore. the heartbreak and tears cannot touch us anymore.

what matters is i AM like you - my father. a poet. who knows silence and the beauty it can bring. a poet. who paints lovely things from broken dreams and childhood memories. a poet. who knows suffering does not last a lifetime. a poet. who always comes back to me. every time i look in the mirror.

mantra

i will not run from the mirror
i will not run from the mirror
i will not run from the mirror

today
is a new day
i will not be afraid
of my shine
i am perfect
just the way i am

my reflection
is one of a kind
i will embrace it
i will breathe
i will walk in truth
i am beyond time

even the most beautiful diamond
is dug from the ground
a star beams bright in the night
it does not make a sound

where i come from
what i have been through
what i am and will go through
is part of my journey

today
i make this promise to myself
to be me and no one else
to love and accept my brilliance

to know that i am different
destined for great things
to make a difference in my life
and the lives of others
to face the challenges each new day brings
with the hope and knowledge
that accepting myself is loving myself

i will not run from the mirror

picadillo is mexican magic

i was in the second grade when i learned how to make picadillo. my daddy taught me. i smile now, remembering. that day, daddy was all mine. i was always daddy's girl.

they called my daddy caloté. it means corn stalk. he was tall and full of magic from mexico. he was a field of dreams. living somewhere in between mexico and america. he was the coolest cat around. everybody loved and feared caloté. when my daddy walked, he commanded respect. he didn't laugh much. he didn't talk much. he didn't have to. his ways were just that. his ways.

he had a way of making my mother swoon. perhaps it was his brown eyes. or, his smile. maybe it was his hair. it hung down to the middle of his back. i just wanted to touch it. all of the time. he always wore dickies overalls and smelled like patchouli.

we lived in a little house. on fairmount street. maybe it was just one bedroom. i can't remember. i was young. so was daddy.

daddy was usually working as a roofer. he'd come home smelling like chiclé and the sun. he always worked hard for us. back then, we didn't know how hard. he was so strong and proud, he made life look easy.

that day, in the small house, daddy was a chef. i was his helper. i remember being confused when he called me into the kitchen. i was always eager to be around him. we started cleaning in silence. we washed the dishes. wiped the counters down. we swept the floor. when we collected the little pile of dirt from sweeping, he asked for a piece of paper. i didn't question him; i just ran to do what he asked. i came back with a sheet of paper from my notebook. what is he going to do with that? i couldn't wait for the magic. he took the paper to the sink. ran a stream of water down one end. he was very careful. the paper dipped and swooned in his hands (just like my mother.)

this! (he said) is a mexican dust pan!

my eyes got wide. i was learning his magic from mexico! i watched completely enthralled as he bent down. he put the wet end of the notebook paper in front of the dirt pile. smoothed out the edges with his finger. he quickly swept the dirt onto the paper. just like that, it disappeared.

i watched my daddy sweep up a lot onto a mexican dustpan. fights with momma. light bills. money orders for the rent. his emotion. memories of his childhood.

what came next was one of the best memories of my own childhood. daddy went to the refrigerator. he took out ground beef. onions, garlic, tomato sauce. a can of mixed vegetables. rice.

he was going to cook! just me and him in the kitchen. cooking for when momma - his prieta, got home. prieta means dark girl. dark beauty. i grew hearing him call momma sweet names like this. she called him 'mi rey' and 'mi vida' and 'mi cielo.' my king, my life, my sky.

i was in the clouds when he started cooking. browning the meat with garlic and onion. secret spices. i studied his every move. he cooked in mostly silence. i wondered if my grandmother rosario taught him how to make this. when he used to live in mexico.

this is picadillo, he said. pouring the can of mixed vegetables into the pot. it was bubbling with water and tomato sauce. and all of the love he put in. the small kitchen smelled heavenly. my daddy made it so.

he made rice. the good, orange-red kind. our kind. with tomato sauce and ajo. con cebolla. con sus propios manos. his own hands.

that night, when our dark-skinned beauty queen came home. there were kisses and smiles. there was a big pot of picadillo, arroz, y tortillas de maíz. he cut some lime wedges. and placed everything onto the table.

i watched him squeeze lime juice into his bowl. i did the same. he put a spoonful of chilé. i did, too. he rolled his corn tortilla in his hand like a map. i did the same. i took a big spoonful of the picadillo into my mouth. i chewed slow. enjoying every drop of my daddy's mexican magic.

he was the first man i ever saw cook. with that pot of picadillo, he honored his family. he made my mother and me happy. i'm sure my brother isaac had some, i just don't remember. i was too busy watching daddy.

i was full for days. even years later, i am still full of his picadillo and mexican dust pan magic.

i made him some picadillo not too long ago. he ate every drop. i smiled like my mother did that day. years ago. in that little house on fairmount street. picadillo is mexican magic. mexican magic is love. it is what my daddy gave me/us.

ask the ground

a few weeks ago. i woke up to find charles working at the dining room table. it was early. shortly after we said our good mornings, there was a knock at the door. a guy from the energy company. he (this camus-looking stranger) wanted to get into our backyard. to see things. to check out the trees. and, their pathways amongst the power lines (existentialism.)

a few weeks before that, i remember saying to charles that they were going to have to prune some of the trees in the field. (not knowing who 'they' were.) the field that surrounds part of our house. not my trees. (who is me?) but, the trees in the field.

i sit with these trees (all of them. mine and field. minefield. mine/feel.) almost every day. i have coffee and meditate with these trees. these trees have covered me. they have become God-like canopy. they have brought me birds and solace. they have become muses.

charles returns to dining room with papers in hand. from across the wooden table he says: baby. they're going to have to cut down our trees.

wait. what?
no. what trees?
our trees.
(i just wanted them to just cut some of the branches. of the other trees. not my trees.)

charles is speaking and i can't hear him.
rainwater is falling down my face.

(am i crying over some trees?)
(yes, i am.)
my oak gets up. consoles me.
we can plant new trees.
they're just going to replant the palm trees somewhere else.
don't cry.

i understand.
(still. not accepting)
not now, he says.
in a few weeks.

okay. i can live with that. i get my coffee and go outside. i
write.
(maybe, everyday since then?)
(since. wind.)

and, forget.
my mind is on my roots.

this past thursday, we get home from natty roots. the royal
reign 7 celebration was a forest. a forest of poets, strangers,
family, dreams come true, hope, laughter, music, spirits, joy,
memory. much more than i could ever attempt to describe.

(how do you describe love?)

charles (my love) notices everything. he sees our gate has
been moved. i go inside while he secures the perimeter. he
comes back and says - they took the trees. the big palm in
front, and two from the back.

(don't look back.)

this morning is my first morning on my back porch. coffee
and clove in hand; i sit them down. there are tree shavings

where i sit. i walk around and notice every branch, stem, tree, bird-sound missing.

i am resolved to sit and write. i look up and say to myself: i can see the sky.

i cannot finish this in sunlight.
(time out.)

i am back.
(some. maybe many. hours/ours. later.)

i have begun to write in the dark.
literally.
(now. and, before now.)
(my writing is changing.)
(is this literature or scripture?)
does that make a difference?

i finish my thoughts now. back on the porch.
in the glory of darkness.
sitting in the middle of hollowed sound and chime.
dreaming of tree root. natty roots & rhyme.
holy ground

question (everything): if a tree falls in the forest
and no one is around to hear it, does it make a sound?

answer (have faith): don't ask me.
ask the ground.

feathers & fruit

(poems)

wind came

wind came
and spoke:
one man's trash
is another man's treasure

rain fell
and said:
wash away
those tears
(what are you crying for?)
fix yo' face.
(for what is coming.)

sand sifted.
through the hour/our glass.
and bellowed:
wait. for no man/woman.
(get up.)
git on 'bout 'yo business.
walk, child.
in/on purpose.

fire burned.
blew us to ashes.
flame said:
flesh of my flesh
bone of my bone
wake up and live
free yourself

we are the universe

123

1) breathe

when the world
takes your breath away
when life beats you down
when you wake up
in the middle of the night
full of worry and what about
when fear whispers in your ear
and fills your head with doubt
when you wake up in the morning
and can't see the light of day
when you collect them pennies
them nickels and dimes
and hope this will be the last time
you swallow your pride
when you hide your face
and stifle the tremble in your throat
when your lifeboat
feels like it's sinking
and you can't stop thinking
about the flood at your feet
when the flood fills your eyes
to the point you cannot see
when one more minute
feels like an impossibility
when one more second of suffering
feels like an eternity
close your eyes one more time
open your mouth one more time
and breathe

2) be yourself

they are the pretty people
they got money
they skinny
they really smart
they going to college
they got jobs
they got better clothes
better shoes
better everything than me
only if i was like them
and nothing like me
they got a house
somewhere to stay
they got money in the bank
they got food in the refrigerator
and in the freezer
they got clean walls
they got everything they want
i got nothing i need
nothing at all
i ain't nothing at all
they got it all
i wish i was like them
they strong
they never fall
i am weak
they not like me
no one is made like you
you are one of a kind
something like a snowflake
made when the winter comes
and the ground is cold
something like a dream
something like a song

something like a light
something so Most High
most everybody cain't see
something so blessing
something so everything
something like no one else
be who you are
not who you could be
be yourself

3) tell the truth

when you talk to the wind
when you talk to them
when you pray
when you write a poem
when you sing your song
when you tell your story
when you testify
when you take a stand
when you wonder
what the world is coming to

1) breathe
2) be yourself
3) tell the truth

and
the world will come to you

in silence

in silence
i watch them
lose themselves
create and recreate themselves

in silence
they watch me
wonder where i came from
why am i here
why do i care

in silence GOD
watches us
like children

we shatter silence
with our words
with our prayers
with our pencils
with our swords
with our songs
with our tears
with our stories

with
each
other

my world is

my world is water
agua/lluvia
rain/reign drop/drop top
top hat/crown of thorns/dreadlocked
natty roots they call me
and i run
circles around words
like time does a tree ring
like tick-tock/never stop
woodstock/tree trunk
poetry/poet tree lines
seed/roots/stems/branches and leaves
watered by you - the things we all go through

my world is water
rooted in rainfall/reign fall truth
the truth is
i am moved by the water
one rain drop/one tear drop
one stream of thought
one mustard seed of faith
one sea/see of dreams
one blank page/one pencil
found in the inkwell of my mind

my world is water
i flow like flood/when i write
one letter/one word
one drop of love/one heartbeat
one poem/one liquid line
at a time
my world is water

girl, stand up

girl, stand up
don't run from your reflection
look into the mirror and see
you are a beauty full thing
something they've never seen
before

they don't make the rules
they don't get to tell you
what to do
or who to be

girl, stand up
be yourself
know you are more than enough
you are a divine being
a star in the sky
a butterfly in the wind
when they talk about you
or laugh behind your back
paint a smile on your face
hold your head high
you are too free and fly
to be held down
by anything that is not light

girl, stand up
don't let them get to you
before you do

young man

young man
with the wondering eyes
and curious heart
moving in and out
of life everyday
dodging bullets
balling out
sometimes struggling
always striving for better days

keep your eyes on the prize
the prize is on the inside
you will win
you get out of life
what you put in

young man
keep your feet on solid ground
keep your mind free
your path is full of light
you are a warrior's song
you are never alone

young man
you are everything you need
keep learning and growing
from mistakes to manhood
love yourself and believe

what lives inside of you
is greatness

lion calling

she enters
the everything
dragging sanguine song
out of god's belly
stardust hanging onto halo/mane
flame will become footprints
divine lion design
killing game
since shine-eye samira
licked river from face
five rocks drew name
from ancestral wind

we rise like roar
to claim the savanna and beyond

she runs
into the everything
heartbeat hunting
running from nothing
blood game blessing
clawing/gnawing
truth from marrow and stones
sweet savage sound feasting
killer bee sting/beasting
hummingbird wing drumming
donkey jawbone crushing
mama earth shattering
prey/pray to ground returning

first law of nature manifesting
the everything is something
flesh cannot see
this spirit calling

the lions are coming

dreams come true

imagine your dream
a small seed
beginning like thought
in your mind
from mind to hand

you hold your destiny
in the palm of your hand
what will you do?
pillage or plant?

do not worry of time
think not of this and that
how or when
trouble talk
will take your seed
with the wind of doubt

believe you me
i have seen the drought
drowned my dream
with what about
made mercy
cry out loud
covered my gift with cloud

fell to my knees
on the ground
saw myself in dirt
all around

it was then

i began to grow
in the not yet and know
know there will be
rocks and rough times
harsh times
make you grow

may you grow a garden
of dreams
dare to believe in harvest

i have seen my thoughts manifest
i know the sweetness of break down
begin again
the caterpillar metamorphosis

most will not read me
they will not get
this truth message

i am speaking to you

if you fail/fall down
find yourself growing
open your eyes and heart

it's not where you've been
it is how you went through

seed-sewing/watering
knowing
within the deepest part of you
is where dreams come true

you can do
all things

leaven/leaving

spirit been starving
been letting babylon
build a tower in my mind
brick by brick
bill by bill
the weeds climb
as high as clouds
meanwhile
belly be sick
mouth a barren field
fingers frantic
blood running panic
both/two feet in fire
four/chambers foot deep
came/coming up
nil/nile river

i am equal parts
madness/mathematical
sacred equation/text
pyramid walking
gods/GOD's talking
i got next

i have dreamed
of mountains running
into water/color
monét
i have dreamed
of brown snakes and concrete ladders
grey matter
i have dreamed

of whales swimming in sky
birds flying in water

the ancestors speak
when i close my eyes
old folk/say
don't nothin' come
to a sleeper but a dream

it seems/seams
i must be both
fin and feather

it seams/seems
i must be both
kunta/kente
cloth

it seems
i must be both
slave and king
drown and drought
i must decipher
things
difference
between
sugar
and
salt

i have dreamed
of crocodile tears
succumbing to sand

i have dreamed
of samira

of giselle
of illegible unchained
of a beauty full muslim woman
pregnant/cloaked in black
named najera
of shining eyes
of the city between rocks
of the unwritten
of so many
of a forest

najera
meaning
treeless country
soy extranjera
above the trees
meaning
I AM
stranger
in my own mind
in my own land

you cannot
will
understand
me
i am
before
i will
destroy
cut down
the tower

i must be
(holy)

babylon letting been
starving been spirit

leaven
leaving

bread
crumbs
labyrinth

i am never lost
even in
my own mind

the freedom of dreams

black baby
gold face
eyes full of blue see

silent stray
dirty feet
wandering spirit
landfilled mind

found
resting place
in darkness of dream
seeking higher ground
like the backside of mountain

within slow rattle mouth shaman
she with peace pipe hands
cupped young ancient

like water from river
and drank
before they both sank
into belly of beast

quiver of arrows
for dispersing shadows
bones quivering
for the below in tomorrow

black baby
with gold face
do you believe?

in the holiness of loneliness?

something sacred here lies
closed-eye kingdom
is inheritance
of faithful orphan

only the silent can speak in tongues
only the young can become ancient

sometimes the discarded
becomes the chosen one

and herein lies freedom

(fin) fin

i am always looking for signs.

i think it is because
i am often lost.
or, feel that way.
i think it is because
my heart beat be rabbit foot
my nose stay to grindstone
or, whatever they say

i think it is because
i am walking cliché
my pencil-lead-body
come up
more short than sharp
my fishing soul/pole
catch more marlin than shark

and, sometimes gawd
eat me/my words up
when i go fishing
in the dark

i am (santiago)
always earnest (ernest)
looking (manolin)
for (his way/hemingway)
signs

you know sometimes
i am more old man
than the sea

sitting on porch (boat)
struggling between

making sense (writing)
(insert mandolin strings)
and
the greatest catch of my life
(breathing)

you know
sometimes
i get gone
(lost at sea)

and, i
drown
one hundred fathoms

down deep
in the water
(of my mind)

where nobody
can catch
(me)

fín
fin

Crown

roots:
in my beginning
i was 817 may street seed
cut from bone/cornerstone
born yellow
in the cold mouth of february
my red/black/and green mother
carried me
my red/white/and green father
painted me

i am sacred sound (dichotomy)
divided between
sunlight and midnight

trunk:
fostered/fathered by grandmother
florene
grounded in wordsoundpower
hadji
i grew (twisted at the root)
helix

i am living proof
black girls make magic
i am revolutionary

fruit:
my words will never done

branches:
may everything
i write
reach sun/light

leaves:

anxiety. depression. post-traumatic . . .
stress (importance of a thing)
(emphasis in the form of prominent relative)
(loudness of a syllable or a word

as a result of special effort in utterance)

disorder. confusion.

crown:

crest. bird's nest. beginning. head.

natural selection. unlocking of keys. the opening of doors. totality.
of above ground's parts. identifying marks. photosynthesis (see:
beyond dark.) energy release (respiration: remember to breathe.)
transpiration (functions performed by/because of leaves.)

jewels: we come/crown into this world. born blessed. gifted with
the breath of life. we grow. we get heavy. we forget. we hold our
mud/breath. we run. we chant. we cry out. we fall down. we get up.
we give. we rejoice. we love.

this is life. the only one we get.

we must remember to honor and water our roots.
we are and have always been. a mighty seed and spirit.
we are forest.

find your purpose, find your crown.

yours, in the journey
natty roots

branching out

(writing prompts)

hate

hate is such a strong word. we are all familiar with the feelings/memories/thoughts the word invokes. think about hate for a few minutes. what do you hate? have you been hated on? do you have a message for your 'haters?' what is the opposite of hate? how has hate impacted your life?

whatever comes to you, write it down.

don't tell me what to write

i was teaching at a private school in houston. these students were hungry and ready to write. i thought about what i had planned. and, i quickly realized, this wasn't the time for plans. this was a time for rebellion and freedom. i saw an empty whiteboard and an opportunity to do something different.

so.

on the board i wrote: don't tell me what to write. and, they went in.

instruction: go in. be free.

12 questions for the universe

we all have questions. we all have the need for answers. i'd like to know where does the butterfly go when it rains? (i didn't come up with that myself. lol. it was the name of a book i read in elementary school. but, it's a good question!)

alright. i'll go first. well, get you started.

1) why do black and brown people suffer so much?
2) how can i forgive those who have wronged me?
3) who is responsible for the earth?
4) can i still turn a cartwheel?
5) when will all of my teeth fall out?
6) do black lives matter?
7) what book should i be reading?
8) can i fly?
9) will they understand me?
10) where do i go when i am sad?
11) how does kendrick write like he does?
12) what will you come up with?

now. it's your turn. number your paper from one through twelve. ask the universe any questions that come. yes, you can write/ask more or less. yes, they can be funny. they can be serious. they can be be whatever you want. just ask.

40 (sacred)

instruction: list 40 people/places/things/sounds/sights that are sacred to you. before you do, look up the word sacred. then, proceed.

for me, some of my 40 would be:

momma. family. music. trees. backporch. daddy. coolspeak. judah. tati. livi. charles. hadji. the fantastics. cheese. wind. rain. sunshine. children. tears. laughter. instagram. my students. the world. writing. poetry. my brothers. dreams. birds. paris. saint lucia. ocean. gi. josh. rock city. my mind.

(whatever it is. write it down. come up with at least 40.)

sidenote: every last one of your 40 (sacred) things is. a poem. blog. post. short-story. all of these sacred things are a part of you.

extra-credit: go beyond yourself.

i looked up into the sky.

instruction: review your 40 (sacred) list. pick one subject/word.

write this up: (never down. everything. every word is for upliftment.)

i looked up into the sky and saw a young star.

i asked the star to speak to me of _____ (insert the word/subject you chose here. examples: family/love/school/my mind/the wind/music/mankind/etc.)

and, the star replied:

(speak/write in the voice of the star. what does the start have to say? listen to your inner self. write it up.)

12 things i love about myself

for some reason, this has been the most-difficult task/writing prompt. seeing ourselves truly. as we should.

i remember. i was a senior in high school. i worked at the dollar-movies on seminary. i was grinding. grinding through the bullying/he/she-said. i was going to school and working. my routine was take a shower. pay one of my brothers to iron my work shirt. while he/they did that. i'd put conditioner in my hair, take a plastic bag from the grocery store and put it on my head. while my hair/crown was doing its thang, i'd get dressed. i'd be in the bathroom mirror. checking myself. one day, my momma passed by and said: get out that mirror! she kept walking.

i was shook. thought the mirror was a bad thing. i realize now, she always knew my beauty. she just didn't want me to get full of myself. she didn't want me to be vain.

this is the thang.

there are things we believe about ourselves. and, then. there are always things that mirror reflects. the mirror reflects the truth.

what i learned then, and want for you/us now is this:

the truth is. it needs no explanation. you just gotta look and see. for yourself.

instruction: list 12 things you love about yourself.
(think inside and out)

sacrifice, gratitude, & honor (letter writing)

my momma sacrificed for me and my family. she was always cleaning, cooking, teaching, preparing us for life. many of these things were not appreciated. we just expected it. i am forever grateful for her. i will honor her by continuing to write our stories. i will continue to teach and learn. i will honor her by carrying on her legacy of love, light, and fire.

who has sacrificed for you? or, who do you make sacrifices for? think about this person or people. what are you grateful for? how will you honor them?

instruction: write a three paragraph letter addressing this special person/people. this could be a teacher/coach/best-friend/grandmother/yourself/anybody.

your first paragraph should be centered on specific sacrifices. second paragraph – gratitude. give thanks for small and great sacrifices they make/have made. third paragraph – how will you honor them?

feel free to add action/color/images/memory. make it personal and heart–opening. it is your choice to share this letter or keep it for yourself.

I AM

I am – list 3 special characteristics about yourself
(examples: loyal, beautiful, and creative)

I see - something imaginary or real

I hear - an imaginary sound

I know - what have you learned about life?

I am - repeat first line or write something new

I love - who or what do you love?
(examples: loud hip-hop, the smell of rain, and my boo)

I live in - literal or metaphorical
(examples: a brick house at the end of the street/the clouds)

I dream - something you dream about

My mind is - (describe or compare)
(examples: a deep blue ocean/like
a labyrinth filled with dreams)

I am – repeat first line or write whatever you feel

what brings wonder?

the world is full of natural wonder. great and small. natural and man-made. the great pyramids, the grand canyon, the great barrier reef, the northern lights. mount everest, lighthouses, waterfalls, statues, trees, gardens, the list is endless. think about it. do some research. choose a natural wonder of the the world. maybe it is a place you've been or always wanted to see. once you have decided, brainstorm. write down what you find. write what you feel and see.

instruction: write a poem/short story/blog/whatever you choose. i challenge you to write in the voice of your natural wonder.

i am sharing what i wrote on the next page. feel free to style-mimic or use as groundwork.

the river nile

have you ever rained/reigned blue and white tears?
have your dreams ever met the sun?
has the pull of the moon ever watered your thoughts?
have the words you have written or unwritten
planted themselves between silt and sand?

sons and daughters
and, everything in between
do you believe you are a natural wonder?
never say never

i began as a raindrop
and, soon became a river
from the mouth of africa
they call me the longest in the world
i am greater than the greatest in the world
still, they come for me

i am ancient
i am mother of blue ink
and, white paper (papyrus)
i have and will
continue to water the greatest kingdoms

i am a natural wonder
i am the river nile

measuring up

i have compared myself to others throughout my lifetime. when i was younger, i was bullied quite a bit. i was too skinny, too poor, too black, not mexican enough, not pretty or fine enough. that's what they used to say about me. honestly, sometimes i feel like i am still not enough. or, i think my writing is not good enough. i don't have enough. the truth is i am enough and so are we all. we are all divine and have everything we need inside.

one day i was thinking about things. things to never measure myself by. i am sharing my list with you. i want you to think about it. add to it. or, write your own.

10 things you should never measure yourself by

10) bills you cannot pay (money is a game)
9) the past (be grateful because it shaped you, but stop looking back)
8) lost opportunities (they were passed up for a reason.)
7) other people (your path is just that. it belongs to only you.)
6) failed relationships (are stepping stones.)
5) fairytales (by definition: marked by seemingly unreal beauty, perfection)
4) moments of depression/anxiety/ptsd (do not define you. help is a reality.)

3) guilt (do not carry it. forgive yourself and others.)
2) religion/society (are man-made. find/nurture your spirit.)
1) unrealistic expectations (you are human. be real with/and LOVE yourself.)

you may even want to create a list of things TO measure yourself by.

heavy is the head

me: momma. i want dreadlocks.
momma: what for? you already got a
crown.

i keep looking at those lines. waiting for
them to seep into my skin like sap. waiting
for inspiration to strike like lightning.
waiting on my spirit to calm. waiting on a
bird to bring me a message from my
momma. from anything. from the wind.

(heavy is the head . . .)

when i think too much, i play in my
head/roots. i pull at my crown. literally, and
metaphorically. and, somehow, jewels fall
out (grace and mercy.)

if you were to ask me: natty, why did you
write this book? what is the purpose of
crown?

i would/wood reply: i don't know. my head
be mixed up. like my blood. (my
eyes/words be flood.)

this book is an offering. a collection of

jewels. a crown of thorns. a drop of
see/sea water for the thirsty soul. a
swallow. salty tears. blue-bird feathers.
grounding. sapling. roots (shall find/follow
me.)

in the beginning was the word. before i
wrote any words in this book. i heard my
bird. felt her feet perched in my crown.

words are where i most find me. (where do
you find yourself?)

crown ain't got nothing to do with royalty.
no kings and queens. nobody above or
below me/us. not for me. crown is different
for everybody/tree. crown got everything
to do with get down (roots.) crown is
always growing up (like trees said.) writing
(like pencil-lead.) dreaming (wind/water
said.)

crown is bird's nest. a seeking. of higher
ground.

heavy is the head . . .

one love,
natty roots

instruction: remember the words i have said.

93

Made in the USA
Columbia, SC
21 March 2019